Everybody Serves Soup

by Norah Dooley
illustrations by Peter J. Thornton

Carolrhoda Books, Inc./Minneapolis

This book is available in two editions:
Library binding by Carolrhoda Books, Inc., a division of Lerner Publishing Group
Soft cover by First Avenue Editions, an imprint of Lerner Publishing Group
241 First Avenue North
Minneapolis, Minnesota 55401 U.S.A.

Website address: www.carolrhodabooks.com

Library of Congress Cataloging-in-Publication Data

Dooley, Norah.
    Everybody serves soup / by Norah Dooley ; illustrations by Peter J. Thornton.
        p.   cm.
    Summary: While trying to earn money by shoveling snow so she can buy her
mother a Christmas present, Carrie comes up with an idea for just the
right gift. Includes soup recipes.
    ISBN: 1–57505–422–1 (lib. bdg. : alk. paper)
    ISBN: 1–57505–791–3 (pbk. : alk. paper)
    [1. Soups—Fiction. 2. Gifts—Fiction. 3. Snow—Fiction.] I. Thornton,
Peter, 1956– ill. II. Title.
PZ7.D7265 Ex   2000
[E]—dc21   00-008091

Manufactured in the United States of America
3 4 5 6 7 8 – JR – 09 08 07 06 05 04

"I love everything about snow. Don't you?" Dad and I were out shoveling the driveway.

"Everything, Carrie?" he grunted a bit. It was deep, heavy snow.

"Oh, yes. I love the smell of the air after it snows. I love snowflakes, snowball fights, snowmen, even shoveling."

"And the snow day you got off school?"

"You bet. Especially before Christmas," I said.

Christmas. I had presents for everyone but Mom. And I was totally out of money.

"What should I get for Mom?" I asked, as we got to the sidewalk. "She always says, 'Anything that comes from your heart is fine.' What is that supposed to mean?"

"You'll think of something," said Dad.

"Dad?" I asked, leaning on my shovel. "Could you pay me for shoveling? And could I go around and see if other people want to be shoveled out too?"

"Don't see why not," said Dad as we reached the street.

I heard a sound like distant thunder. It was getting louder and louder.

"Oh no! Look!" I said.

"It's the plows!" said Dad, jumping back and pulling me with him. In a few seconds, the whole driveway entrance was covered again.

"The city giveth and the city taketh away," said Dad with a tight smile. So we shoveled more heavy snow. When we were done, Dad said, "That was a job worth overtime pay." And he put a ten dollar bill in my mitten.

"Yes!" I said and gave him a quick hug.

I looked down our street at the fences, cars, and garbage cans. They were covered with foot-high piles of snow that looked like white cakes.

Boosh! A huge wet snowball hit me in the back of my head. I whipped around and saw Tito peeking from behind a car. He was laughing and making another snowball.

I pretended to bend down to shovel, but I came up with a snowball. It got him right on his neck and slid inside his coat.

"Hey!" Tito brushed snow from his collar. "Could I borrow a shovel?"

"For what?" I asked. You just never know with Tito.

"I want to do my house," he said.

"Okay, I'll help," I said, getting my father's shovel.

We shoveled a path down the sidewalk, up his steps, and onto his porch.

"Hey, let's go get paid," I said.

"Who's going to pay us?" said Tito. "The landlord won't. He doesn't even live here."

"Whoops, I forgot," I said as I blew into my mittens to warm my hands.

"Never mind. We can go upstairs and get warm. Fendra is making soup."

Upstairs, Tito's sister Fendra had a huge pot on the stove. She was taking sips from a ladle. "Yo, Carrie, what are you doing?"

"I'm trying to make money to buy a Christmas present for my mom."

"Me too," chimed in Tito.

"As if," said Fendra, ladling out some soup for us. "What are you going to get, Carrie? I got my mom some bath oil and lotion."

"I never know what to get. I want it to be special. My dad is no help. He always shops on Christmas Eve and buys whatever."

As we sipped soup, Tito said, "I'm going to get Ma a Lincoln Continental Town Car and a diamond necklace."

"Tito. Be real, just get her something this year."

"This is delicious soup, Fendra," I said, changing the subject.

"My abuela taught me to make it—the one in Puerto Rico. I got the ham hock and the okra, herbs, and pigeon peas at the Spanish store in the square."

"My mom would love the recipe. She loves soups."

"I can give it to you right now," said Fendra. While she talked, she wrote on the back of an envelope. At the kitchen stove, the snow had melted off our boots and made a puddle.

"Come on," said Tito. "We'll never make any money sitting around talking about food."

Fendra handed me the envelope, and we took off.

The smell of lemon and chicken soup stopped us at John's apartment door. Tito said, "Let's get John too."

Anna, John's older sister, answered the door. "Yeah, guys?"

"Can John come out and shovel with us?" we asked together.

"He's got a cold, but you can come in and say hello."

John was at the table with a huge bowl of soup in front of him. His mother was at the stove.

"Hi, Mrs. Stephanopolis," I said. "That smells great."

"It is very good for a cold," said John's mother.

Tito started to cough—what a faker. I nudged him with my elbow, but Mrs. Stephanopolis was already pouring two small cups for us.

"Thank you," we said. We drank and chatted with John.

"What a bummer to be sick on a snow day," said Tito.

"This is so good—what's in it?" I asked John's mother.

She started telling me lots of ingredients, and John handed me a piece of paper. I wrote as quickly as I could.

"Thank you," I said, after I stuffed the paper, with the envelope from Fendra, into my pocket. Tito was in a hurry to make money, so we said good-bye and ran outside. There was just a dusting of snow on what we had shoveled before.

Down the street, we saw Mark sweeping off his father's ancient blue car.

"Can we help?" we asked as we got closer. Mark just grinned as he swept a broom full of snow in our faces.

The window above opened, and we all looked up. Mark's mother said, "Don't forget to do the steps too, Mark."

"Yes ma'am," he said.

We all started to shovel like mad, throwing snow high over our shoulders.

"Hey," Mark said. "Watch it. You might get some snow on someone."

"Like this?" I asked, throwing a load onto his shoulders.

"Yeah, or like this," Mark said, taking a broomful and dumping it on my head.

Soon we all looked like snow people. We stopped to catch our breath.

"Let's work together this time," said Mark.

"It's got to be a neat path," I said to Tito as we shoveled. "Otherwise no one is going to pay us."

"Nobody's going to pay us anyway. I don't get paid 'cause I owe my mom money," said Mark.

"It was too much fun to get paid for it anyway," I said.

"I'm freezing," said Tito.

Mark's mother looked out again. "Nice job, y'all—once you got to it. Now, come on in before you turn to ice cubes."

We took turns brushing each other off, then we tromped upstairs.

"Now, what is the coldest on you?" asked Mark's mother. "Looks like your nose, Tito, and your hands, Carrie. Mark! Didn't I tell you to wear a hat? Your ears are about to fall off with the cold," she said, putting her hands on Mark's ears.

"Ha!" said Anne-Marie. "He's funny-looking enough already." Then she slammed her door shut when Mark started to chase her.

"That's enough from you all," said Mrs. DeLoach, and she motioned us into the kitchen.

"Here's a bowl of corn chowder for each of you. We used to make this down home when it got cold—at least we thought it was cold."

The chowder warmed us inside and out. Tito and Mark started to have a contest to see who could eat more bowls of soup. I stopped after one bowl and looked down at the front of our house. My mom and my brother and sister, Anthony and Anna, were at our window. I thought I should go and check in with them. Tito and I said thanks and hurried downstairs.

"We're not exactly making our fortune on this street," said Tito. "I'm going to see if I can make some serious cash where more people have driveways."

"Okay. But bring back the shovel," I said.

Anna and Anthony had colds, so they had to stay inside and do Legos and stuff. They peeked from behind the door until Mom shooed them away.

"Carrie, where have you been all morning?"

I told her.

"Then I guess you don't need any lunch," Mom said. "Would you like to go see if Mrs. Ambrose and Crystal need anything?"

"Sure," I said.

From the alley I could see a tall teenage girl was shoveling Mrs. Ambrose's steps. I introduced myself and started to help shovel.

"I'm Ambrose's grandniece," the girl said. When I asked if they were home, she said, "Go on up."

The door was open, and I ran up the stairs, snow falling off my boots with each step.

"Sure smells good in here, Mrs. Ambrose." Their kitchen had a spicy and rich aroma. "What are you making?"

"Child, what you smell is oxtail soup. And this, behind you, is Darlene, our grandniece." Darlene had come up the stairs, sweeping the snow I'd left behind.

"She's going to the store for us," said Crystal. "Can you just show her the way from the corner?"

"Sure," I said. "Let's go."

Darlene said she was from Barbados. I loved her accent.

"This is my first time to see snow," said Darlene. I tried to imagine what that would be like. As if reading my mind, Darlene said, "It's prettier but colder than I imagined."

At the corner of our street, I said, "It's right down there," pointing toward the square where all the stores are, and we waved good-bye. Turning around, I noticed Wendy Shinzawa struggling to push a huge ball of snow. The Shinzawa family is new on the block.

"What are you making?" I asked Wendy. "Can I help?"

"Okay." She said it so quietly I could hardly hear her. She's really shy.

We made three snowballs in a row—big, bigger, biggest. When we ran out of snow, I cleared her sidewalk and driveway. Wendy was piling clumps of snow on the snowballs. An enormous snow dragon took shape right in front of my eyes. We were hot from all the work, and our cheeks were red.

"Wendy, you are an awesome artist. Wait 'til I show Anthony and Anna," I said. Wendy turned even redder with embarrassment. Her mother knocked on a window and waved us in with a smile.

"You work hard," Mrs. Shinzawa said from their front door. "Please come in and be warm."

"Thank you," I said. "We did it to make the sculpture, really."

"Do you like miso soup?" Wendy asked me.

"I don't know," I said.

Mrs. Shinzawa showed me to their table, where there were four covered wooden bowls and two pairs of chopsticks. "Please," she said, pointing for me to sit in a chair.

"Thank you." Under the wooden cover, the soup smelled like nothing else I'd ever eaten. Wendy picked up the bowl and drank right from it as she held her chopsticks, so I did too. In the other bowl was very sticky white rice. It was delicious.

Mrs. Shinzawa gave me a shaker that had some flaky green stuff with sesame seeds in it. "Seaweed," she said, after I tasted it and liked it.

We ate without speaking, and I had a minute to think about my mom's present. I wasn't making much money, but I was starting to get an idea.

"Can you tell me how you make this?" I asked.

When Mrs. Shinzawa didn't know the English word, she showed me the ingredients. Wendy helped translate as I wrote on the back of a leaflet about supermarket specials. I had a plan.

"Good-bye, Wendy! Thanks, Mrs. Shinzawa! See you!"

I decided to stop by Mrs. Max's. I wanted her advice.

"So Carrie, out in the snow and with your shovel?" Mrs. Max said, smiling as she opened the door.

"Hi, Mrs. Max," I said. "I'm out trying to make money by shoveling snow so I can buy my mom a present."

"What a shame, the janitor has shoveled so soon."

"Yeah, I haven't made much money, but what do you think of my idea for a present?" I said as I pulled the papers from my pocket. "See, these are soup recipes. I could make my mother a collection of soup recipes from the neighborhood for Christmas. Do you think she will like it?"

"Very clever. But these you will wrap as a present?" she asked, pointing at the papers. She thought for a minute, then she opened a drawer and pulled out a pretty little book with unlined pages.

"You could make her pictures and recipes in a book like this."

"That's what I was thinking. Did you get this at the stationery store in the square?" I asked.

"Yes," said Mrs. Max. "Inside this one I have a recipe for my beet and cabbage soup. Would you like that?"

Before I could answer, Mrs. Max looked out the window. "Oh!" she said. "I see it is nearly dark, and I must light the candles for Hanukkah."

I was surprised that the streetlights were on already. I needed to be home soon. Mrs. Max took a small candle down from her mantelpiece. She said a prayer, then she lit one candle, and with that one, two others.

While we made the soup, Mrs. Max told me about Hanukkah, and I told her about our Advent wreath.

"This is great. I have a list of neighbors to get soup recipes from, and I already have some of the recipes. Thank you. Do you think my mom will really like it?"

"Of course. Remember, Carrie, it is said that good soup with a friend warms more than the body. Your mother will love it."

It was dark as I walked home. The snow sparkled in the streetlights. The sky had cleared, and I could see some stars.

Anthony answered our door. "I got to light the Advent wreath! And we made lentil soup and fresh bread for dinner. Did you make a lot of money?"

"Let me in, Anthony. I have the best idea for Mom's present. Everybody was so nice, and they were all making soup," I said. I pulled him into my room where Anna couldn't hear. She can't keep any secrets. I told him about filling a blank book with pictures and recipes.

"But what about money?" said Anthony. "We'll still have to buy the book, won't we?"

"I've got ten dollars from Dad, and besides, you couldn't buy the kind of thing we're going to make. It's just what Mom would want. It's not just soup. It comes from the heart."

Recipes

Fendra's Abuela's
Puerto Rican Chuletón

Pigeon peas are also called gandules or gungo peas or congo peas. You can buy them in Latin American grocery stores. If you can't find them, you can substitute canned navy beans.

1	large ham bone with meat
6	cups water
2	large onions, chopped
1	teaspoon turmeric
½	teaspoon cumin
½	cup rice
3–4	potatoes, peeled and finely chopped
3–4	carrots, peeled and finely chopped
1	can cooked pigeon peas
	salt and pepper to taste
	cilantro (fresh coriander), chopped

1. In a soup pot, cover ham bone with water. Add onions, turmeric, and cumin. Bring water to a boil. Then reduce heat and simmer for one hour, until meat has fallen off the bone.
2. Remove ham bone.
3. Chill soup until fat hardens on top. Skim fat off the top of the soup.
4. Bring soup back to a boil. Add rice, potatoes, and carrots. Reduce heat and simmer for 20 minutes.
5. Add pigeon peas, heat through, and salt and pepper to taste. Top with cilantro.

Mrs. Stephanopolis's
Chicken Soup with Lemon
(Avgolemono)

6	cups chicken stock (or broth)
2	onions, chopped
2	cloves garlic, minced
1	carrot, chopped
2	bay leaves
½	cup orzo or rice
3	eggs
	juice of one lemon (about ¼ cup)

1. Bring chicken stock to a boil. Add onions, garlic, carrot, and bay leaves. Reduce heat and simmer for 30 minutes.
2. Remove bay leaves.
3. Add orzo to the soup. Continue to simmer for 20 minutes, until the orzo is cooked.
4. Use a wire whisk to beat eggs and lemon juice together in a small bowl. Slowly pour about ½ cup of the soup into the eggs and lemon juice, stirring constantly.
5. Slowly pour the egg and lemon mixture into the soup. Continue to cook over low heat, stirring constantly. Keep stirring a minute or two as the soup thickens.

Mrs. DeLoach's
Southern Corn Chowder

2–4 slices bacon
2 onions, finely chopped
3–4 cups water
6–8 potatoes, peeled and chopped
2 packages frozen corn
1 quart whole milk
salt and pepper to taste

1. Cook bacon over medium heat in bottom of soup pot until barely crispy. Take out bacon and chop into small pieces.
2. Pour out all but a tablespoon of bacon grease from the soup pot. Sauté onions in remaining bacon grease for 5 minutes.
3. Heat water in a teakettle.
4. Add potatoes to the onions, cover with warm water, and bring to a boil. Cook for 10 to 15 minutes until potatoes are tender.
5. Puree the soup in batches in a blender.
6. Return soup to pot and add corn. Cook for 3 or 4 minutes. Add milk and bacon, and carefully heat without boiling. Salt and pepper to taste.

Mom and Anthony's
Italian Lentil Soup

3 tablespoons olive oil
2 onions, chopped
3 cloves garlic, chopped or pressed
6 cups vegetable stock
1 large can tomato puree
1 teaspoon oregano
½ cup parsley, chopped,
   or 2 tablespoons dried parsley
1 sprig rosemary, chopped,
   or 2 teaspoons dried rosemary
2 cups green lentils, washed
   grated Parmesan or Romano cheese

1. Sauté chopped onions and garlic in oil in soup pot.
2. Add vegetable stock, tomato puree, oregano, parsley, rosemary, and lentils.
3. Bring to a boil, reduce heat, and cook for 30 to 45 minutes, until lentils are tender. Stir occasionally. Add water while cooking if necessary.
4. Garnish with grated cheese.

The Shinzawas' Miso Shiru

You can buy kombu seaweed and miso (fermented soybean paste) in Asian grocery stores or health food markets.

6–8	inches kombu seaweed
6–8	cups water
½	pound tofu, cut into ½-inch cubes
3–4	leaves Chinese cabbage, finely sliced
1	leek, finely sliced
4–6	mushrooms, finely sliced
4–6	tablespoons red or brown miso
	soy sauce

1. Bring water to a boil. Add kombu seaweed and continue boiling for 3 to 4 minutes. Remove seaweed from pot. (The stock you have made is called dashi, Japanese soup stock.)
2. Add tofu, cabbage, leek, and mushrooms to the dashi. Boil for 2 to 3 minutes. Reduce heat.
3. In a separate bowl, add ½ cup of dashi to miso. Stir to dissolve miso.
4. Add dissolved miso to soup and turn off heat. Do not boil miso soup once the miso has been added.
5. Add soy sauce to taste.

Mrs. Max's Beet and Cabbage Soup

Be very careful cooking with beets. They stain easily!

3	tablespoons canola or vegetable oil
2	onions, chopped
2	cloves garlic, finely chopped or pressed
3	cups vegetable stock
1	small medium-sized red cabbage, chopped
3–5	beets, sliced or cubed
2	tablespoons lemon juice
	salt and pepper
	sour cream or plain yogurt

1. Heat oil in soup pot. Sauté onions and garlic until onions are transparent.
2. Add vegetable stock, cabbage, and beets. Bring to a boil, reduce heat, and cook for 10 to 15 minutes, stirring occasionally, until beets are tender.
3. Puree soup in batches in a blender.
4. Return soup to pot and reheat.
5. Salt and pepper to taste. Serve hot or cold with sour cream or yogurt garnish.

Mrs. Ambrose's
Barbados Oxtail Soup

You can find oxtail, the tail of an ox, in the meat section of the grocery store, or your butcher can order it for you. It is often cut into sections.

1	oxtail (about 2 pounds)
2	tablespoons vegetable oil
2	onions, chopped
½	teaspoon salt
8–10	cups water
4	whole cloves
1	teaspoon curry powder
½	teaspoon cinnamon
4	potatoes, peeled and chopped
4	carrots, peeled and chopped
2	tablespoons lime juice
	salt and pepper
	fresh parsley

1. Heat oil in soup pot. Add oxtail, onions, and salt, and brown oxtail on all sides.
2. Cover oxtail with water and add cloves. Bring to a boil, reduce heat, and simmer for 3 to 4 hours, until meat falls from bone. Add water, if necessary, to cover oxtail.
3. Remove bone from soup. Chill soup until fat hardens on top. Skim fat off the top of the soup.
4. Reheat soup. Add curry powder, cinnamon, potatoes, and carrots. Simmer for 15 to 20 minutes, stirring occasionally, until vegetables are tender.
5. Add lime juice, and salt and pepper to taste. Garnish with parsley.